Text and illustrations copyright © 1997 by David McPhail.
All rights reserved. Published by Scholastic Inc.
Printed in the U.S.A.

ISBN 0-439-45162-0

16 15 14 13 12 11   23   11 10 09

The Great Race

by David McPhail

SCHOLASTIC INC.

New York   Toronto   London   Auckland   Sydney
Mexico City   New Delhi   Hong Kong   Buenos Aires

All of the barnyard animals
were bored.

"Let's have a race," said the cow.
"Where?" asked the duck.

"Let's race around the world,"
said the goose.
"That's too far,"
said the rooster.

"Around the barnyard,"
said the pig.

The animals lined up
at the barnyard gate.
"When do we start?"
asked the duck.
"When I say go,"
said the dog.

The rooster started to run.
"You said go," he called,
"so I'm going!"

The other animals ran after him.
First the duck, then the goose,
the cow, and the dog.
The pig was last.

But the pig tripped and fell.
He rolled downhill . . .

past the goose, the duck,
the cow, and the dog.

He rolled right on top
of the rooster.
"Ooofff!" said the rooster.

The other animals stopped
to see if anyone was hurt.

"I'm fine," said the rooster.

"I'm dizzy," said the pig.

The race continued.

As the rooster ran past the henhouse,
the hens cheered loudly.

But he slipped in the mud.
So did everybody else.

All but the pig.
He was used to running
in the mud.

The pig passed the other animals.
The race was almost over.

"Puff, puff, puff,"
went the pig.

"Clomp, clomp, clomp,"
went the cow.

"Pant, pant, pant,"
went the dog.

The duck, the goose, and
the rooster used their wings
to go faster.
"Flap, flap, flap."

And the animals reached
the gate at the very same time.

"I won!" cried the duck.

"Me, too!" said the goose.

"So did I!" said the cow.

The rooster bowed.

"I'm the greatest!"

"I'm top dog,"
said the dog.

"I'm a champ,"
said the pig.

And they all were very happy
as they walked off to rest.